THE GREAT
FATHER
CHRISTMAS
ROBBERY

Scholastic Publications Ltd,
10 Earlham Street, London WC2H 9RX, UK

Scholastic Inc.,
730 Broadway, New York, NY 10003, USA

Scholastic Canada Ltd,
123 Newkirk Road, Richmond Hill,
Ontario L4C 3G5, Canada

Ashton Scholastic Pty Ltd,
P O Box 579, Gosford, New South Wales,
Australia

Ashton Scholastic Ltd,
165 Marua Road, Panmure, Auckland 6,
New Zealand

Published by Scholastic Publications Ltd, 1991

Text copyright © Terry Deary, 1991
Illustrations copyright © Stuart Trotter, 1991

ISBN 0 590 76606 6

Typeset by AKM Associates (UK) Ltd, Southall, London
Made and printed by Cox & Wyman Ltd, Reading, Berks

THE GREAT FATHER CHRISTMAS ROBBERY

Terry Deary

Illustrated by Stuart Trotter

Hippo Books
Scholastic Publications Limited
London

When you're ripping open presents at the break
of Christmas Day,
Don't forget the kind old man in red and white.
Don't forget the man who brought you all that joy
and happiness.
While you slept he worked so hard all through the
night.

You may think he has an easy life just dropping
off your toys,
You may think he has to work just once a year.
But old Santa has had problems of the sort you'd
never guess,
Open up this book and read of them in here . . .

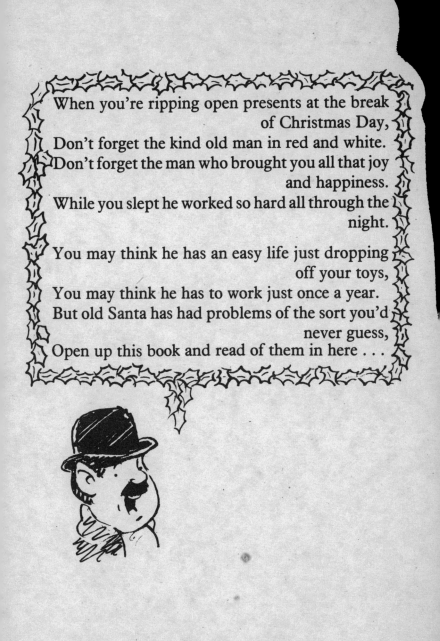

'Twas the night before Christmas Eve, and all through the house, something was stirring . . . and it wasn't a mouse!

Or even a moose!

More like a reindeer.

I stuck my head out of my bedroom window and looked up. There, on my roof, was a reindeer, chewing my television aerial. And behind the reindeer a sleigh loaded with presents. It was just like a visit from Father Christmas . . . but why was he a day too early?

I crept downstairs and peered around the living room door. There he was! A fat little feller with a bushy white beard, a poppy-red suit and dark glasses. He was filling his sack with some of the presents that lay under the Christmas tree. I know I should have gone back to bed, but I was so thrilled at seeing Father Christmas that I hid and watched.

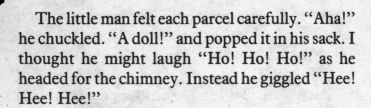

The little man felt each parcel carefully. "Aha!" he chuckled. "A doll!" and popped it in his sack. I thought he might laugh "Ho! Ho! Ho!" as he headed for the chimney. Instead he giggled "Hee! Hee! Hee!"

I tiptoed back to my bed. I lay down. I jumped up. Hey! That fat little man was *filling* his sack. He wasn't *leaving* presents . . . he was *stealing* them. I looked out of my window just in time to see the thieving Father Christmas and his thieving reindeer fly off into the night with a "Hee! Hee! Hee!"

"Help!" I cried. "There's a pair of nickers on my roof!"

I knew the police could never catch them – not unless I called the flying squad.

Someone who looked like Father Christmas was out to ruin the day for all the children. Someone had to stop him . . . someone like me! But where did I start? Where would I get help? Where were my clean socks?

This was a case for that great detective . . . Sherlock Gnomes!

I looked up his number in Yellow Pages . . .

GNOME & AWAY
Soap Manufacturers   Australia 321

GNOME & DRY
Towel Manufactures   Bath 123

GNOME MOST THINGS
School   Eton 213

GNOME SICK
Hospital for little people   Illverness 231

GNOME WORK
Builders for gnomeless people   Brixton 312

GNOMING PIGEONS
Messenger Service   Nestminster 321

GNOMES SHERLOCK
Greatest living detective   Clueless 123

HOLMES SHERLOCK
Greatest dead detective   Baker St 21b.

I called the great man at once . . .

I waited five hours! Suddenly there was a tap on the door.

I peered through the window and saw a funny looking little feller . . . deerstalker hat, hooked pipe under his chin and a violin smouldering in his mouth.

I opened the door and there stood the famous Sherlock Gnomes. The great man himself . . . just like in the pictures . . . but smaller.

I quickly told him my story . . .

"TWAS THE NIGHT BEFORE CHRISTMAS AND I SAW FATHER CHRISTMAS COME DOWN THE CHIMNEY AND PINCH ALL THE PRESENTS WHAT DO YOU THINK?"

I THINK . . . YOU'VE BEEN ROBBED.

BUT BY WHOM?

BY FATHER CHRISTMAS OF COURSE.

HE WAS WEARING DARK GLASSES. I'LL NEVER BELIEVE THAT FATHER CHRISTMAS GOES ROUND STEALING! COULDN'T IT HAVE BEEN A THIEF DISGUISED AS FATHER CHRISTMAS?

NO! IT WAS FATHER CHRISTMAS DISGUISED AS A THIEF.

AMAZING MY DEAR GNOMES!

ELEMENTARY MY DEAR WATSON.

So we set off on the trail of Father Christmas. Snow drifted up to Sherlock's chin – it wasn't very deep. We didn't have snow shoes but we strapped a couple of tennis racquets onto our feet.

"Sorry I don't have the real snow shoes," I told him.

"Never mind," the great man sighed, "these racquets will have to serve."

I wouldn't have known where to start searching for a burglar but Sherlock insisted on following tracks along the road. . . .

The great detective was right, of course. What else could leave deep straight tracks in the snow and jingle along like that?

Well, a tram for one thing! But a man like Sherlock Gnomes isn't the sort to be put off by a battered nose and a broken violin.

We limped after the tram and caught it as it stopped for a zebra crossing. Luckily for us the zebra took its time. I bought two tickets for the North Pole and sat down for the long cold journey.

As we rattled along Sherlock told me his cunning plan. He decided that we needed to know more about this Father Christmas character. Where did he come from? How did he get the job? And what made him turn crooked? But, for Sherlock the most burning question of all was . . .

Luckily we found a snack-bar that was open . . .

SAM 'n' ELLA'S SNACK-BAR

Bacon & Penguin Eggs   1.00 (clean plate 20 extra)

Deep-Fried Igloo   1.00 (per bottle)

Reindeer-food   10.00 (per bag - vely deer indeed).

Frozen chips   1.00 (home-grown mashed potato)

M'whale Burgers (in whale fat)   1.00 (for cry babies - eat them + blubber)

Ice burgers   1.00 (A Titanic snack)

Turkey Soup   1.00 (For gobblers)

Eskimo Milk   1.00 (From eskimoos)

Ice Cream Surprise   1.00

TRY ELLA'S SPECIAL POTATOES! SHE CROSSED A POTATO WITH A SPONGE - THE POTATO TASTES AWFUL. BUT IT'S GREAT WHEN YOU MOP UP YOUR GRAVY!

So we knocked on Ella's door . . .

I wouldn't say Ella's snack-bar was scruffy but I'll swear I saw a skunk with a clothes-peg on its nose. There was a lot of food on the menu . . . and even more on the tables and the floor!

"That soup looks like dishwater!" I complained.

Ella gave a sickly grin. "Oh, dear!" she cried.

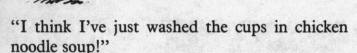

"I think I've just washed the cups in chicken noodle soup!"

We sat at a table with a spotted cloth – spots of stale food mostly – and ordered.

SHERLOCK:	Ella! Ella! This egg's bad!
ELLA:	Don't blame me! I only laid the table.
SHERLOCK:	Then give me two Ice Cream Surprises!
ELLA:	Surprise! Surprise!

Sherlock Gnomes wasted no time in questioning the woman . . .

So we left the snack-bar and set off on the search for the real Father Christmas and to solve the mystery of the missing dolls. We had just twelve hours to find a thief and return the loot. Twelve hours to save Christmas for all the children in the world!

The North Pole houses were more cheerful than Ella's cafe. Brightly painted wooden cottages with carved shutters keeping out the cold wind. We found Grandfather Claus's house thanks to Sherlock's amazing powers of deduction again. (His name was printed inside the wellies that

stood on the doorstep!) It looked lovely and warm in that cottage.

Grandfather Claus was a jolly old man. So old that even his wrinkles had wrinkles. He was fat, but not so fat as an elephant, and his nose was red – but not so red as an elephant either. As we went in a cat jumped down from his lap. He asked us to put the cat out – I hadn't even noticed it was on fire!

"What brings you to the North Pole?" he asked.

"A tram!" Sherlock said quickly.

SHERLOCK:	We've come to ask you about your son.
GRANDFATHER:	Me *Sun*? I never read it! I only read the *North Pole Times*.
WATSON:	No! Your s-o-n. Son!
GRANDFATHER:	Ah! You mean our Santa Claus!
SHERLOCK:	Is that what you call him? How did he come to get a name like that?
GRANDFATHER:	I'm glad you asked me that. It's a funny story . . .

So he told us . . .

"Not a lot of people know this, but Santa Claus was born at a very early age. In fact he was born a full twelve months before his first birthday. An unusual baby, though. It was the white beard and whiskers that did it . . ."

WHAT DO YOU THINK OF HIM DOCTOR?

LET'S SEE . . . . . WELL! HE'S THE MOST UNUSUAL BABY I'VE SEEN FOR A LONG TIME. LOOKS THE SORT OF BABY THAT COULD GROW UP TO BE THE NEXT FATHER CHRISTMAS!

"We were so proud!" Grandfather Claus told us. "And Santa was a wonderful baby! Everybody loved him. We entered him for the 'North Pole Beautiful Baby Competition' and, would you believe it, he won!"

DID HE WIN EASILY?

NO. HE WON BY A WHISKER!

But we still wanted to know how he got the name Santa Claus . . .

Grandfather Claus told us it was all due to a mistake at the christening. It seems the vicar was deaf as an on-duty traffic warden. At the same time Grandmother Claus was worrying about what to send her Auntie Gladys for Christmas.

VICAR: I name this child . . . er . . . .

GRANDMOTHER: What shall we send Aunt Gladys?

VICAR: I name this child . . .

GRANDFATHER: Send her clothes!

And that was how Father Christmas got his name! Of course Grandfather Claus wasn't too happy about it, but it was too late to change it. Santa was stuck with the name.

He smiled as he remembered, "Still, it could have been worse."

"How?" Sherlock asked.

"You should have seen what happened to the next kid they gave him for christening!" the old man chuckled.

"What happened?" I asked.

"Well, his mam had drunk a bottle of pop before she went to the church . . ." Grandfather Claus explained.

Grandfather Claus told us that Santa Claus was the most popular boy in the school. . . .

Well, it isn't every day you share a desk with a white-bearded friend, is it? Of course !Burp! Pardon was white-bearded too – but !Burp! was the nastiest, meanest white-bearded boy you'd ever wish to meet. He could look after himself. The other kids were scared of !Burp!. While they were playing harmless games like pulling the legs off snails !Burp! was doing much nastier things – like pulling the legs off dolls!

Grandfather Claus went on, "Then one day the school caught fire. The kids escaped by climbing down Santa Claus's beard to safety. After that he was a hero in the school. Everybody loved him. Everybody except one . . . !Burp! Pardon was jealous!"

WATSON: Did this all happen in his junior school?

SHERLOCK: They didn't have junior schools in the old days, Watson.

WATSON: So what sort of school did he go to?

"I think we need to see Santa's teacher," Sherlock murmured.

"She's called Miss Taycon . . . and she lives just across the street," the old man told us. "But be careful!" he warned. "She can be a bit touchy . . . and when she starts swinging her stick you have to duck pretty sharp!"

"Sherlock Gnomes is afraid of no one!" the detective said dramatically. "He boldly goes where no bold man has boldly gone before . . . boldly!"

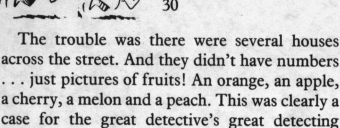

The trouble was there were several houses across the street. And they didn't have numbers . . . just pictures of fruits! An orange, an apple, a cherry, a melon and a peach. This was clearly a case for the great detective's great detecting powers.

"Which one, Sherlock?" I asked.

"The one with the melon, Watson," he answered.

"Amazing, Sherlock. How could you possibly know?" I gasped.

"Melon-entry, my dear Watson," he smirked.

And, of course, he was right! When I knocked on the door an old lady answered. She was wearing a mortar board and gown and carried a cane.

I was terrified. I felt ashamed, but I had to admit it.

"I'm terrified, Sherlock!" I whispered.

"I'm not!" the bold detective said . . . boldly.

"How can you stand there so calm and unafraid?" I gasped.

"Easy," he replied. "I'll just stand behind you! If she's going to hit someone then it's more likely to be you!"

"Thanks," I muttered and turned towards the towering teacher.

Eventually she let us in. We sat by her roaring fire and listened as the old lady remembered her days at North Pole Elementary School.

"Now, Phil McCavity became a famous dentist," she boasted.

"How famous?" Sherlock dared to ask.

"The best in the world. That's why they call him 'Leader of the Plaque'," she told us. "Then there was the brilliant inventor – Noah Lott," she went on, "he crossed a bed with a microwave oven. Now he can get eight hours' sleep in ten minutes."

I made the mistake of trying to interrupt her. "Miss Taycon . . ."

"How dare you!" she roared and drilled a hole in my chest with that stick of hers. "Noah was never mistaken." And the old teacher went on to tell us about the great inventor. "He invented an upside-down lighthouse."

Sherlock asked who would want an upside-down lighthouse!

"Someone in a submarine!" the teacher told him.

This was all very interesting, but we had just eleven hours left to save Christmas! We had to find out more about the man we'd come to find.

SHERLOCK:	Er . . . madam . . . could you tell us about Santa Claus?
TEACHER:	Became a chimney sweep or something, didn't he?
SHERLOCK:	I think you're mistaken.
TEACHER:	Of course I'm Miss Taycon – always have been!

But at last she remembered the boy with the white beard. The trouble was she didn't think much of his school work.

"Brains of a brick," she said. "Didn't he pull the legs off dolls?"

"No," I told her.

Then she went to an old cupboard and found a pile of school reports.

"Here we are!" she cried. "Claus, Santa!" and pushed the report across to Sherlock Gnomes. The great detective peered at it through his magnifying glass . . .

NORTH POLE ELEMENTARY
End of Term Report

PUPIL   : CLAUS, SANTA
FORM   : 1T
NO. OF PUPILS IN CLASS: 47

ENGLISH	: Rites good poems but carnt spell.	21/100
HISTORY	: Carnt tell a Norman from a gnome.	11/100
MATHS	: MENTAL -3/50 PROBLEMS -3/50.	TOTAL 6/100
GEOGRAPHY	: Thinks Greece is what you fry chips in	16/100
SCIENCE	: Made anti-freeze by putting her in fridge	19/100
P.E.	: Keeps tripping over his beard.	
TOTAL	:	Not a lot

POSITION IN CLASS: 46
TEACHER'S SIGNATURE: Miss Taycon.
HEADTEACHER: Should go far. The further the better.

I. Canem

"Ah, yes . . ." she smiled, "I remember the boy now!" And Miss Taycon told us of some of Santa's problems in lessons.

"But he was good at poetry, the report said," I reminded her.

"Ah, yes! Wonderful poems he could write!"

"AN OLD MAN WENT DOWN TO THE SEASIDE;
A FAT LITTLE FELLER CALLED KELLY.
HE WALKED IN THE SEA FOR A PADDLE,
TILL THE WATER CAME UP TO HIS KNEECAPS."

Santa's old teacher smiled at the memory of her second-worst pupil.

"I wonder whatever became of him?" she asked.

"He became Father Christmas," I told her.

Miss Taycon nodded briskly. "Ah! I knew he had *something* to do with chimneys. Of course he was very kind and very popular! Now I come to think of it he wrote me a poem when he left the school . . . a sort of 'thank-you' poem. I still have it on the wall."

She pointed to a framed sheet of paper that hung on her wall. I read the moving poem . . .

To my Favourite Teacher - Miss Taycon.

My Teecher you're kind and you're cuddly,
at teeching us kids you're a winner.
I like you much more than my pet pussy-cat
And I like you much more than school dinner!

My teecher you're ever so clever
You teeches us how to rite poems.
You teeches us two and two makes three or four
And how Italy's a big town in Rome

My teecher knows all about naycher,
How plants grow and why the bees buzz.
You never gets mad even when we are bad,
Oh, how does you put up with uzz?

I'll miss the old school now I'm leaving.
My poor little heart it is breakin'.
I'll miss all me friends but my love now I sends
'Cos mostly I'll miss you Miss Taycon.

The teacher wiped a tear from the corner of her
eye and sniffled into a handkerchief.

Sherlock opened his mouth to ask a question, but I jumped in first.

"And can you remember what sort of pupil !Burp! Pardon was?"

"What do you want to know about him for?" Sherlock sighed. "He has nothing to do with our case."

"I'm not so sure, Sherl," I told him. "A boy who could write a poem like that could never grow up to be a thief!" I turned back to the teacher. "Do you remember !Burp!?" I asked.

"Ah, yes. If Santa was second-worst in 1T then young Pardon was the very worst. At least Santa was a kind, gentle boy. But !Burp! was wicked! Did you know he used to pull the legs off dolls?"

"We have heard," I said. "Was he as stupid in class?"

"Not stupid!" she snapped. "Awkward!"

The teacher shook her head. "And !Burp! was always late. I once asked him why. He said it was because there were eight in his family – and the alarm was only set for seven! Another time he said he was late because his father ran over himself that morning. Of course I was very concerned so I called to see !Burp!'s dad and he explained. His dad had asked !Burp! to run over to the shops for a loaf of bread. !Burp! refused . . . so his dad had run over himself!"

Sherlock sighed. "Very interesting, I'm sure, but not very important."

"Sorry, Sherl," I muttered.

"Don't call me Sherl," Sherl said.

"Sorry, Sherl . . . er, Sherley."

"And don't call me Shirley!" he moaned, steam coming out of his pipe.

"Sorry, Sherl . . . ock!" I smiled.

He turned to the old teacher and asked, "What we really want to know is what happened to Santa Claus when he left school?"

Miss Taycon drew a deep breath through her channel-tunnel nostrils. "He became a right little tearaway!"

"No!" I gasped. "Surely!"

"Don't call me Shirley!" Sherlock screamed.

"No! No! No!" I said quickly before he pushed

his magnifying glass into my big mouth –
sideways! "I meant *surely* Santa didn't turn bad!"

Miss Taycon shrugged her large shoulders.
"Got in with a bad crowd – with that !Burp!
Pardon's gang!"

"A gang! What did they do?" I asked.

"They dressed in leather clothes . . ."

"They bought some two-stroke, twin-cylinder
sleighs . . ."

"They fitted supercharged reindeer . . ."

"And they raced them round and round the
North Pole!"

"No one was safe on the roads!"

(!!Important Footnote!! Penguins do *not* live at the North Pole – they live at the South Pole. But you sometimes get a lost penguin wandering around and kindly nuns take them home! OK? That's sorted that out. Now we can get on with the story.)

"No one could sleep at night for the jingle and the clangle of the harnesses."

"Their name struck terror into the heart of every polar bear north of the Sahara desert!"

"They were . . ."

I asked Santa's old teacher how his days as a Bell's Angel ended. Seems he had a nasty accident once.

Santa escaped with just a bruised beard . . . but the reindeer was a write-off.

THE REINDEER WASN'T KILLED I HOPE?

NO, BUT IT GOT TWO BLACK EYES!

SOUNDS LIKE A BAD-EYE-DEER.

SO SANTA WAS A ROAD HOG?

MORE LIKE A SLEDGE HOG! BUT THE CRASH PUT AN END TO HIS WILD DAYS!

Miss Taycon told us how sorry Santa was about the crash. He never forgot how to drive a speeding sleigh – and that came in useful later! But he has always been kind to his reindeer ever since.

What I wanted to know was, what happened to !Burp! Pardon. But Sherlock asked, "What did Santa do after his crash?"

"Luckily he found himself a nice girlfriend and settled down . . . she lives just a few doors down. Why not pop along and see her?"

We had just nine hours left to save Christmas
... but Santa's girlfriend might be able to give us
a clue. We had to go.

"Her name is Helen . . . Nellie for short!"

We dashed to the door.

"But, Sherl!" I cried. "We don't know where
she lives!"

But the great detective hurried down the street
and into a cottage with "H" on the door.

"Helen-entry, my dear Sherlock," I muttered,
"I should have known!"

A cheerful old lady answered the door and
grinned. Her cheeks were as rosy as a tomato and
her teeth as yellow as best butter. Her white hair
was pulled back in a bun – it was a bread bun and
the crumbs were falling down her back.

"Here! I know you!" she cried.

Sherlock blushed.

"You're that famous detective! I've seen you
on the telly!"

"Well, madam . . ." Sherlock began.

"I think you're brilliant! Eeeh! Wait till I tell
my friends . . . I've met Agatha Christie."

Sherlock sniffed. "Actually, I'm *not* Agatha
Christie – I'm the famous Sherlock Gnomes –
I'm on the trail of the even famouser Santa Claus.
I wondered if you could answer some questions!"

"Come in, come in!" she smiled and led the way into her small cosy cottage. On the mantelpiece stood a picture of Santa himself.

"You were a friend of his?" I asked.

She sighed. "My very first boyfriend! Every time he saw me in the street he used to run and hide!"

"He did?" Sherlock asked.

"Well . . . he was very shy as a young man," she explained.

"But at last I sent my pet dog out to catch him and bring him back. A cute little hound called Buttercup!"

DON'T WORRY THE DOG'S A VEGETARIAN. HE ONLY EATS GREENGROCERS!

She explained that all she wanted was one of Santa's famous poems.

"And he wrote one for you?" I asked.

"Eventually," she cooed. "After I'd locked him in the garden shed for two days without any food! Ahh! He was so shy!"

"Hmm!" Sherlock muttered. "Have you still got this poem?"

She took it lovingly from a drawer and spread it on the table in front of us. It wasn't one of Santa's best – and the handwriting was very shaky.

"He must have been *very* shy when he wrote this. Nervous even!"

Nellie nodded. "Probably because Buttercup was smiling at him!"

I read the poem . . .

LOVE POME TO NELLIE.

I know a young lady, her name it is Nellie,
And each time I see her me knees turn to jelly.
It could be her smile, or her nose red and wet. . .
Or it could be the dirty great teeth of her pet!

I know a young lady, a wonderful sight,
Her teeth are like stars — 'cos they come out at night
Her love is as great as the princess and frog. . .
So I'll hop it when I get away from this dog.

I know a young lady she's fat and she's fair
And my heart strings are tied — like my legs to this chair.
I'll never leave Nellie, her slave I'll become. . .
At least till her doggie lets go of me bum!

Santa Claus.

"Er . . . very moving," I said.

"Yes," Nellie sniffed. "So sad. So sad. He's dead, you know!"

Sherlock jumped to his feet. "Impossible! Santa can't be dead!"

Nellie looked at him blankly. "Not Santa . . . Buttercup, stupid."

"Oh!"

"He ate someone that didn't agree with him," she sighed. Then she looked up brightly. "Would you like to meet my new dog?" she asked.

I beat Sherlock to the door by a centimetre. "No thanks!" I said quickly. "Just tell us what happened to Santa!"

"Oh, he got a job," she shrugged. "I remember seeing it advertised in the *North Pole Times* . . . everyone said he should apply for it. They said he was a natural, what with the whiskers and all that!"

"What sort of job was it?" Sherlock asked.

Nellie took another scrap of paper from the drawer and pushed it across the table to us.

WANTED!

A white-bearded person to do the job of Father Christmas!

Must be a good sleigh driver

51 Weeks' holiday a year

Free uniform – provide your own reindeer.

No pay but lots of gnomes to help

Single people only need apply

Apply to: Old Father Christmas

Ice Palace, The North Pole.

WANTED!

"Of course Santa applied. He knew it meant we could never be married – but he made that great sacrifice because he loves helping people!" Nellie explained.

"So, Old Father Christmas was retiring, was he?" I asked.

Nellie nodded. "He only does quiet jobs now – like sitting in shops in December and dishing out presents to children. He's too old to do all that flying around!"

"So, Old Father Christmas gave the job to the thieving Santa Claus, eh?" Sherlock guessed.

"I'm not sure," I began.

"Santa wasn't very bright," Nellie admitted, "but he was never a thief."

"He is now!" Sherlock snapped. "Docker Watson here saw him with his own two ears, didn't you, Doc?"

"Well, I . . ."

"Let's go and see the Old Father Christmas. See what made him trust a toy nicker. Always thought he was Saint Nickerless!" Gnomes went on, sucking his pipe.

"He still lives in the Ice Palace," Nellie told us. She told us a lot more. She told us so much that we thought we'd never get away. At last the desperate detective leapt to his feet.

"Let's go, my dear Watson!" Sherlock cried.

"We've only got seven hours left to save this Christmas."

"Cup of tea before you go?" Nellie asked.

"Please!" I said.

"Lemon?"

"No, thanks, I never eat raw lemons! Yeuch!" I told her.

"No! No! No!" Sherlock groaned. "Not tea *and* a lemon . . . lemon-*in*-tea, my dear Watson!"

And so we made our way to the palace of Old Father Christmas.

It was a fabulous palace made entirely of ice! The tourists loved it! – but the sparrows weren't so keen. Every time they landed on the roof they slid off!

And it was an absolute nightmare for window-cleaners!

WONDER HOW THOSE TOWERS ARE FASTENED TO THE WALLS?

SAME WAY AN ESKIMO HOLDS HIS HOUSE TOGETHER.

HOW DOES AN ESKIMO HOLD HIS HOUSE TOGETHER?

IG-GLUES IT OF COURSE!

We stood at the mighty Ice Gate to the palace and wondered how to get in.

"Tap on the door, Watson!"

"Can't do that, Sherlock."

"Why not?"

"Because we did that joke on page 12!"

"Then jingle his bells!"

The door was answered by a maid on ice-skates.

"Is Old Father Christmas at home?" Sherlock asked.

"Eh?" the maid asked, cupping a hand to her deaf ear. Unfortunately the cup was full of hot tea.

"He said is Old Father Christmas at home?" I shouted.

"A gnome?" she said. "No! Old Father Christmas isn't a gnome – but he has some gnomes working for him."

The old maid passed us each a pair of ice skates and said, "Follow me!"

Sherlock pulled the skates on and sighed, "I like to slip into something comfortable now and then!" Just as he said it he slipped into an icy wall! Ouch! Great detective – awful skater.

The maid showed us through the icy palace till at last we came to a comfortable sitting room. She offered to announce us.

"Who shall I say is calling?" she asked.

"I'm Docker Watson . . ."

"There's a doctor to see you, Old Father Christmas!" she yelled at the old man in the red, fur-trimmed coat.

"Ah good! Doctor! Doctor! My kidneys are bad. What should I do?"

"Take them back to the butcher," Sherlock suggested. "Now breathe out sharply three times."

"You want to check my lungs?" the old man asked.

"No! I want to clean my magnifying glass," the great detective told him.

"But I can't keep food down. Everything I swallow keeps coming up!" Old Father Christmas complained.

"Then quick! Swallow my football pools!" Sherlock cried.

It took us a long time, but at last we convinced him that we weren't doctors and got down to the point of our visit.

"We're trying to find out the truth about Santa Claus – he's been pinching presents," Sherlock explained.

"Oh, dear!" the old man exclaimed. "Doesn't sound like him at all!"

"Docker Watson here saw it all!" Sherlock said sadly.

"I thought you said he wasn't a doctor! I have this problem with my red suit . . ."

"Don't start that again," I groaned.

"I keep wanting to wear a gold suit instead!" the old man said.

"Just a gilt complex," Sherlock snapped. "Now tell us how you came to employ this villain Claus!"

"Well, it all started when I decided to retire, a hundred years ago – we Father Christmases live a very long time, you know. To tell the truth I was getting too old and fat to get down the chimneys."

"Don't tell me," I muttered, "it didn't soot you any more?"

He ignored me. I don't really blame him.

He went on, "I put an advert in the *North Pole Times*. Only two people applied."

"Santa Claus was one," Sherlock said smugly.

"How did you know?" Old Father Christmas gasped.

"I'm a detective," Sherlock shrugged, "I guessed."

"And the other one was . . ."

"!Burp! Pardon," I put in quickly.

"Amazing!" the old man said. "Are you a detective too?"

"No. I'm a docker!"

"Then, doctor, maybe you can tell me why I feel so dog tired!"

"How long have you felt like this?"

"Ever since I was a puppy!"

"But tell us about the interviews," Sherlock cut in.

"Ah, yes. The interviews. I interviewed !Burp! Pardon first . . . I asked him if he liked children."

LIKE THEM? I USED TO BE ONE!

Old Father Christmas thought it was a bit odd that he said his favourite toys were dolls.

"I remember, he didn't own a reindeer, which could have been a problem. Seems he had had one but it crashed and broke an antler."

| OLD FATHER CHRISTMAS: | You'd need a reindeer for this job. |
| !BURP!: | That's alright, I'd hire one. |

HOW DO YOU HIRE A REINDEER?

STAND IT ON A TABLE!

"I was tempted to give him the job . . . but he wasn't as pleasant as young Santa Claus . . . and I thought his dark glasses might scare the kids," Old Father Christmas explained.

"The thief that I saw was wearing dark glasses!" I told Sherlock.

"Aha! A clever plot by Santa Claus to put the blame on !Burp! Pardon, see?"

"Er . . . no! I don't see," I muttered.

"So how did you come to hire this Santa character?" Sherlock asked.

"He seemed so keen to do the job he dashed straight out and bought a second-hand reindeer . . ."

"Santa explained that he knew nothing about reindeer and honest Arfur said he had just the animal he needed. That was the first time Santa Claus set eyes on his famous friend, Rudolph!"

Of course Santa was hopeless at sums, Old Father Christmas explained, but he did notice that the reindeer had a very red, shining nose.

And Arfur Chance went on to describe how Rudolph came to get his red nose . . . .

Arfur explained that Rudolph was a very famous reindeer. One day his owner had been taking a short-cut across a frozen pond when the ice cracked and the sleigh slipped in.

Rudolph tore himself free and galloped off for help as the sleigh was slowly sinking. He couldn't

use the phone to call help so, instead, he galloped up to the top of the church tower and rang the bell – an alarm bell.

The fire brigade rushed out and saved the sleigh . . . but Rudolph was left with a badly battered conk.

So Santa bought Rudolph the red-nosed reindeer . . . but couldn't afford to have his nose re-sprayed. Old Father Christmas told us that it's been that way ever since.

"But, Sherlock!" I said excitedly. "The reindeer on my roof – the one that flew off with my presents! It had a *black* nose!"

"So?"

"So . . . it wasn't Rudolph!" I cried.

But Sherlock had the answer to that. "Everyone knows that great criminals use stolen cars for bank robberies. Santa must have used a stolen reindeer for a toy robbery!"

"I suppose so," I agreed glumly. After all –
Sherlock was the world's greatest living detective.
Still, I couldn't believe that the great poet and
popular young Santa could have grown up to be a
thief.

"And Santa Claus took over from you?" the
detective went on.

Old Father Christmas nodded. "Had to train
him first, of course . . ."

But Old Father Christmas wasn't going to give up
that easily . . .

Old Father Christmas chuckled as he remembered that trick. But then he sighed and said, "Maybe that's what went wrong. Maybe after a hundred years of getting it right he's getting it backwards."

"I see!" Sherlock said. "*Taking* the toys instead of *giving* them! Elementary, my dear Watson."

But I shook my head. "Then why didn't he take *all* of the toys? How come he only took the dolls?"

"Ah! Oh!" Sherlock spluttered. "You didn't tell me that!" he objected.

"I thought I did. Maybe I forgot," I mumbled.

He pointed his magnifying glass at me and said, "You'll never make a great detective. First you suspect the innocent !Burp! Pardon – and then you forget things!"

"Sorry, Sherlock . . . where to next?"

"Er . . . I've forgotten!"

Old Father Christmas said, "If I were you I'd pop down to the gnomes' toy workshop. They'll be all ready to load up in time for Santa leaving . . . three hours from now. If they don't know what's become of him then no one will!" That didn't leave us much time! We had to get going again immediately!

Sherlock jumped to his feet. "Just what I was going to suggest. We'll interview the gnomes and chat to the reindeer!"

"Oh, Sherlock!" I laughed. "You can't chat to the reindeer! You're talking through your hat!"

"Of course I am!" he grinned. "It's a deers-talker hat!"

There was no answer to that.

The kind old man offered us food before we went. "Have a cake!" he offered.

"Thanks!" I smiled.

Old Father Christmas rang a bell. "The cakes were baked by my maid."

"Wonderful!" Sherlock cried. "I *love* gnome-maid cakes!"

So, full of tea and cherry cake, we set off down Reindeer Road to the Father Christmas work-shops. But time was short – nearly as short as Sherlock – and it was growing dark!

Father Christmas's workshops were set in a huge log building. There were a dozen doors or more and outside each one stood a sleigh, loaded with sacks. Not a gnome was in sight.

"Which door shall we try?" I wondered. Each entry had letters above it. "A/B Entry", "C/D Entry" and so on.

"Different entries for different countries," Gnomes explained.

"Don't tell me!" I said suddenly. "Let me guess!" And I headed for the door with L/M above it.

Sherlock nodded, but before he could say anything I beat him to it. "L/M Entry, my dear Sherlock!"

"Correct!"

I knocked. From behind the door came a frightened voice.

"Who's there?"

"Docker!"

"Doctor Who?"

"No. Not Doctor Who, I'm Docker Watson!"

"You can't come in!"

"Why not?"

"Because you may be the great toy robber!"

Sherlock stepped forward. "I am the famous Sherlock Gnomes. I can solve anything!"

There was a muttering behind the door then another voice said, "Then solve this riddle . . . What is green, made of concrete and grows in fields?"

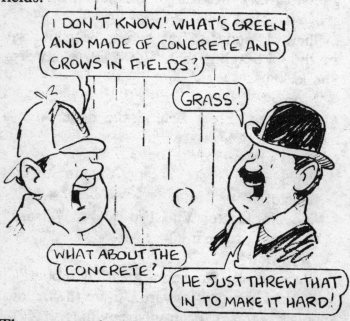

> I DON'T KNOW! WHAT'S GREEN AND MADE OF CONCRETE AND GROWS IN FIELDS?

> GRASS!

> WHAT ABOUT THE CONCRETE?

> HE JUST THREW THAT IN TO MAKE IT HARD!

The gnomes let us in and dragged the great detective to a stool by a roaring log fire. Each one had his or her name on the front of their green overall.

"You have to help us!" Gnorman groaned. "Two hours to Christmas Day and Father Christmas is missing!"

71

"I can't help you!" Sherlock gasped. "I'm too old to climb down chimneys!"

"Santa Claus is older than you!" Gnora the Gnome pointed out.

"Ah!" Sherlock said. "But he's had stacks of practice!"

"We don't want you to take his place," Gnigel the Gnome said. "We want you to find him! Otherwise we'll have to give all the dolls away to the kidnapper!"

"Kidnapper!" Sherlock scoffed. "What makes you think he's been kidnapped?"

"We've had a note," Gnora the Gnome said, and she pushed it into Sherlock's hand.

Dear Gnomes and Dear Deer,

I have your Father Christmas. He is My prisoner. Bring me all the dolls in your factory by midnight on Christmas eve or Christmas is cancelled this year! I will be waiting in the house of that kind old man! Burp! Pardon.

You have been warned!

Ron Buppard

BUT THIS IS BLACKMAIL!

PROBABLY COS HE DROPPED IT DOWN THE CHIMNEY!

"See, Sherlock!" I cried. "Ron Buppard! Rearrange the letters of Ron Buppard and what do you get?"

"Er . . . Barr Up Pond?" he suggested.

"No! It's !Burp! Pardon!"

"But !Burp! Pardon can't be the Great Toy Robber," he objected.

"Why not?"

"Because he's a kind old man . . . it says so in the letter!"

Which just goes to show. Even the world's greatest detective can be pretty thick sometimes!

I dashed to the door. "Follow me!" I called to Sherlock and the gnomes.

I jumped on the sleigh with the red-nosed reindeer hitched up while the others piled on the sledge pulled by a cross-eyed reindeer.

It was a long drive to !Burp! Pardon's house and
Sherlock became bored. So he rummaged in one
of the toy sacks and came out with a book to read.

"What are you reading?" I asked.

"The tale of the princess and the frogs!"

"I thought it was just one frog . . . the princess
kissed it and it turned into a prince!"

"No-o!" Sherlock said. "This is different. In the first story the princess kissed a stupid frog."

"What happened?"

"It turned into a tadpole!"

"What about the next story?"

"That's about the greedy princess. She married a rich old frog then just waited for him to croak!"

At last we reached a lonely cottage standing in a field of snow. Moonlight glinted on a loaded

75

sleigh, piled with sacks. And every sack was overflowing with dolls.

"We'll have to be careful!" Sherlock whispered as we pulled up by the lighted window. We peered over the sill into the little room. A fire blazed in the hearth, and there was Santa Claus – tied to a chair with a white-bearded man in dark glasses sitting in front of him. !Burp! Pardon. The one who pinched my presents!

"You see!" I hissed. "!Burp! Pardon *is* the villain! It's only half an hour to midnight. !Burp! pulls the arms off dolls. What will he do to Santa Claus?"

"You could be right, Watson!" Sherlock admitted.

"Santa Claus is just an 'armless old man," I moaned.

"He will be if we don't rescue him!" the Great Detective said grimly. "We need a plan!"

"Rush in and free him!" I suggested.

"Don't be stupid," Sherlock snapped.

"What do you suggest?" I asked.

Sherlock thought as precious minutes ticked away. "I think . . . we should rush in and free him!"

"Great idea!" I urged.

Sherlock slipped around the corner while I watched through the window.

Two minutes later the great detective returned.

Suddenly !Burp! Pardon's voice carried through the window. "Twenty minutes, Santa!"

Santa shook his sad old head. "Ah, !Burp! Why are you doing this?"

"So that no one in the world can have a doll for Christmas!"

"But why? Why? Why?"

"Because, when I was a little boy, no one ever let *me* have a doll for Christmas! They said that boys can't have dolls! So I tore the legs off all the girls' dolls – if I couldn't have one then they couldn't have them either! See!"

"That's mean," Santa said.

"I don't care. And soon I'll have all the dolls in the whole wide world! That'll fettle them!" !Burp! cried.

"But if you don't set me free then *no one* will get a present for Christmas this year!" Santa pleaded.

"And why should they?" !Burp! sniffed.

"Because we always give presents at Christmas," Santa said gently.

"Since when?"

"Since nearly two thousand years ago . . . haven't you ever heard the story of the first Christmas?" Santa asked. When !Burp! shook his head Santa went on, "I once wrote a poem about it. Do you want to hear it?"

!Burp! nodded. "You always did write great poems, Santa!" he said, and unfastened the ropes that held his old school mate.

Santa rubbed his wrists. Sherlock, the gnomes and the reindeer and I all gathered around the window to listen as Santa recited his story . . .

THE FIRST CHRISTMAS

The shepherds were watching their flock in the fields

While stars in the dark sky were flitting.

Thomas was carving a fine wooden doll . . .

While young Jim got on with his knitting

. . . a scarf.

As Tommy remarked, "That's a big star up there!"

An angel came down with a bound.

Old Tom dropped the doll and young Jim dropped a stitch . . .

While the sheep ran around and around

. . . in circles.

The angel just folded his wings and he grinned,
"Halo, lads! Get along to the tavern!
A baby is born, it's the child of the Lord!
Take some prezzies and let the babe have 'em . . .
please."

"We cannot do that! You great feathered fool!"
Old Tom stood and started to shout.
"The sheep'll get got by the greedy old wolf!"
But the angel said, "I'll sort him out! . . . don't
worry."

But still the old man he was fussing about.
"I haven't got no gifts at all!"
But Jim said, "I'll take the young baby me scarf,
And you, Tom, can give it the doll. . . if you like."

The Angel said, "That's very kind of you lads,
But don't forget Joseph and Mary."
So Jim said, "We'll take them a nice little lamb –
That one there is all cuddly and hairy
. . . and fat."

The shepherds went trotting down Bethlehem
Hill

And they followed the star where it shines.
"Look at that!" Tommy cried, "There's three
camels down there!

And they've parked them on two yellow lines
. . . they'll be for it!"

Now the shepherds felt shy as they crept in the
back

Of the stable and saw who it were!
Three great kings standing there with their arms
full of gifts,
Stuff like gold, frankincense and some myrrh
. . . very posh!

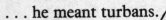

Jim's small lamb it went "Baa!", mother Mary
said, "Ahh!
Come on in! Put your gifts by the bed."
Tommy said, "Sorry, lady, our gifts aren't so
grand
As them blokes with the towels round their
heads!"

. . . he meant turbans.

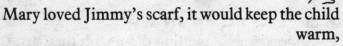

Mary loved Jimmy's scarf, it would keep the child
warm,
And the lamb's wool could make her a frock!
"In fact, Joseph," she said to her husband that
night,
"We could even start up our own flock
. . . think of that!"

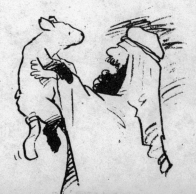

(Now Joseph just smiled and he said, "Very
                                        nice,"
But the truth was his smile was a sham.
To be honest he'd looked at the gift and he'd
                                        thought,
"Tasty chops – or a nice leg of lamb!
... yum, yum, yum!")

Poor old Tommy felt sick as a six-year-old chip,
As he held out his wood doll so sad.
"Sorry, lady," he groaned, "but the chap with the
                                        wings,
Never mentioned the babe was a lad
... he won't want dolls!"

Mary smiled very kind at the shepherd so old
And the wood doll was really quite beautiful.
"It's the thought, not the gift, that's what
matters," she said.
"And who knows, but it might come in useful!"
. . . she was right.

Meanwhile, back in the palace, bad King Herod
had heard
Of a new king and he was real cross.
So he sent out his men for to find him and snatch
him,
And make jolly sure he got lost
. . . for good!

When the shepherds returned to their sheep in
the hills,

Leaving Mary and Joseph in danger,
Twenty soldiers burst in to the stable that night
And they snatched up the babe from the manger
. . . that was that!

But Joseph just laughed and his wife Mary smiled
As she slipped the babe from her cloak's creases.
And the soldiers so dim never knew to this day . . .
'Twas the wood doll that they'd chopped to pieces
. . . served them right!

So when Christmas time comes we remember the
first gifts
From good kings and shepherds in tatters.
And the words of the lady so wise when she said,
"It's the thought, not the gift, that's what
matters."
. . . Merry Christmas!

And Santa Claus finished his poem as the clock creaked around to midnight. The only sound was the soft sniffle of !Burp! Pardon.

"What did you say happened to the doll? Chopped to pieces!" he sighed.

"Turned out to be a valuable gift after all – even for a boy, didn't it?" Santa Claus smiled.

"Poor doll," the gnome in the dark glasses groaned.

"I thought you hated dolls – pulled their legs off," Santa argued.

"Only out of spite – only 'cos no one let me have one," !Burp! muttered miserably. "I hate to think that I'm as rotten as that nasty Herod! Poor doll!"

"Ho! No!" Santa said cheerily. "There'll always be plenty of dolls . . ." then the smile slid from his face, "except this year, of course."

Midnight started to strike.

!Burp! Pardon looked at Santa guiltily. "It's Christmas morning! The children will be waking up in a couple of hours . . . and finding their stockings empty!" he murmured.

Santa nodded sadly. "Even if I set off now I'd be struggling to make it before morning. Not without some help!"

"I'll help!" !Burp! cried. "My sleigh is outside . . . and I'm faster than you!"

As they hurried out into the snowy night Sherlock and I slid back into the shadows.

"Look!" Santa cried. "Here's my Rudolph! And all of my gnomes! With your help, !Burp!, we might just make it!"

Santa and !Burp! jumped aboard their sleighs. With a cry of "Hi-ho, Rudolph, away!" and a jingling of bells they rode off into the night.

So Sherlock Gnomes had saved Christmas for the children – with a little help from me, Docker Watson, and a lot of help from Santa's Christmas poem. The trouble was we were stuck at the North Pole.

KNOCK! KNOCK! WATSON

WHO'S THERE SHERLOCK?

WENCESLAS!

WENCESLAS WHO?

WENCESLAS TRAM BACK TO FELIXSTOWE?

I THINK WE'VE JUST MISSED IT!

I asked, "How do we get home, Gnomes?"

Even the great detective didn't have the answer to everything. "Walk, I suppose."

And we set off to walk back to Felixstowe. There was snow on the ground, snow in the sky

and snow as far as the eye could see. But, with the great Sherlock Gnomes for company, I was never bored.

"I spy with my little eye something beginning with 'S'." I said.

After just half an hour Sherlock had guessed it. "Snow!" he exclaimed.

"Amazing, my dear Gnomes," I gasped.

"Elementary, my dear Watson," he shrugged.

"But how did you guess?" I asked.

"Because I am the world's greatest detective," he smiled.

I shook my head in wonder at the great man's talent. "My turn," he said as we came to the edge of a forest full of Christmas trees. "I spy with my little eye something beginning with 'S'."

"Er . . . snow?"

"No."

"Er . . . Sherlock?"

"No."

"Er . . . six-ton sausage roll?"

"There isn't one," Sherlock pointed out.

"No – but if there was I'd eat it all," I groaned. "Alright, Sherlock, I give up. What do you spy with your little eye beginning with 'S'?"

He pointed at a fir tree. "Shrub!"

And the world's greatest detective and I went home for a cup of tea . . . sitting by a Christmas tree loaded with presents for the kids.

Santa had made it after all.

So now you know how Christmas almost ended
with no toys,
How the children nearly woke up to disaster.
But thanks to Father Christmas and his gnomes
(and Rudolph too)
He whizzed around the world just that bit faster.

Remember, then, that Christmas time's not fun
for everyone.
So don't just think of getting – think of giving.
If people cruel or jealous try to make your life too
hard,
Then you should try forgetting – and forgiving.